WHAT IF DINOSAURS WERE PINK?

BY JARRETT WHITLOW

ILLUSTRATED BY DANIELA DOGLIANI

ISBN: 978-1-943258-84-0

Edited by Jessica Carelock

Warren publishing

Published by Warren Publishing
Charlotte, NC
www.warrenpublishing.net
Printed in the United States

To Ella, Chase, and Luke
For your inspirational imaginations,
and for questioning EVERYTHING!

– JW

Did you ever stop to think,
"What if dinosaurs were pink?"
There are a whole lot of unknowns,
considering all we've found is bones.

All we've ever heard is that they're green,
and several types were kind of mean.
We know they were big, and laid eggs to have babies,
but if you really think about it, there are still a lot of maybes.

Maybe they got dressed up all the time
to play with friends 'til eight or nine.
I bet they wore huge, fancy shoes
while they busted out their funky dance moves.

Maybe they loved to sing songs so cheerful,
instead of just roaring and making others fearful.
Perhaps their tails acted like propellers,
and maybe T-Rexes were excellent spellers.

Maybe they lived in great big houses,
and were quite scared of little mouses.
It could have been they all had professions,
like lawyers, doctors, or teachers of lessons.

Maybe they went to school and did lots of homework,
but got out every summer—an excellent perk!
They may have worn braces to straighten their teeth,
or slept in beds, unafraid of monsters beneath.

Maybe they had spots like a Dalmatian.
You can picture it too, if you use your imagination.
Some scientists think they may have had feathers
to keep them warm in various weathers.

Maybe they drove cars and watched drive-in movies,

or wore underpants to cover their dino booties!

We'll never know if they laughed loud as ever,
or knew how to juggle, play football…whatever.

There's no evidence any of these things exist,
but our great scientists continue to persist.
Once buried, not much lasts through the years,
although they may search their entire careers.

The searching is difficult, the digging is tough,
but we may find the answers if we dig deep enough.

Meanwhile it's fun just to imagine
what could have been during the dinos' time in action.

Perhaps one day we'll know and not just think
how cool it was that dinosaurs were pink.